P9-CQY-470

# WALT DISNEY's
# Cinderella

DISNEY
PRESS

New York

Once upon a time, there was a beautiful
girl named Cinderella. She lived with
her stepmother and two stepsisters
in a house in the country.

Cinderella's stepmother was a cruel woman
who made her cook the meals ...

... serve everyone breakfast in bed ...

... and feed the animals!
But Cinderella never
complained. She made
friends with the animals
and was always happy.

The King knew it was time for his son to get married. He decided to hold a ball and all the eligible women in the kingdom were to be invited.

When the invitation arrived at Cinderella's
house, her stepsisters were very excited.

Cinderella's mice friends made her
a beautiful dress to wear to the ball.

But the jealous stepsisters tore it to pieces.
Now Cinderella had nothing to wear.
She could not go to the ball.

As Cinderella wept in the garden, there appeared a kindly fairy. "I am your Fairy Godmother," she said.

With a flick of her wand, Cinderella's rags became a beautiful gown, and glass slippers appeared on her feet. "The spell will wear off at the stroke of midnight," warned the Fairy Godmother.

The King was happy that so many people had come to the ball. But the Prince did not like any of the girls that were there.

At last, Cinderella arrived. As she entered the room, everybody stopped to admire her beauty.

The Prince fell in love with her, and they danced all night.

Oh, no! Cinderella forgot the time! As the clock struck midnight, she ran away from the palace as fast as she could. In her haste, Cinderella left behind a glass slipper.

As the spell wore off, the coach became a
pumpkin, and the horses became little mice. All
that was left of Cinderella's magical night was the
glass slipper she still wore on one foot.

The Prince declared that he would marry the woman who fit the glass slipper. At once, the King sent his guards to find that woman.

Cinderella's stepmother did not want her to try on the slipper, so she locked Cinderella in her room.

Both stepsisters put on the glass slipper.
But, try as they might, the slipper wouldn't fit.

Just as the guards were about to leave, Cinderella's mice friends helped her escape from her room.

She tried on the glass slipper …
A perfect fit!

The guards took Cinderella to the palace. The Prince married her straight away, and they both lived happily ever after.